Black Lagoon® Adventures

SPECIAL EDITION #1:

HUBIE COOL: VAMPIRE HUNTER

Get more monster-sized laughs from

The Black Lagoon®

Black Lagoon® Adventures

SPECIAL EDITION #1:

HUBIE COOL: VAMPIRE HUNTER

by Mike Thaler

Illustrated by Jared Lee

SCHOLASTIC INC.

To Emily, my niece—a blood relative
—M.T.

To my wife, PJ, who I love necking with
—J.L.

INVISIBLE
COOTIE
↓

Text Copyright © 2015 by Mike Thaler
Illustrations Copyright © 2015 by Jared Lee

ISBN 978-0-545-85075-9
10 9 8 7 6 5 4 3   20 21 22 23

Printed in the U.S.A.   40
First printing 2015

Z

← STAR
SLEEPING

CONTENTS

← HOG BUG

CHAPTER 1
A GRAVE SITUATION

I moved silently through the cemetery. I was amazed that all these people had been alive at one time . . . and some of them still were!

I clutched a steak in my right hand. It was a sirloin, medium rare, and it was the only way to kill a vampire.

"Stop daydreaming, Hubie."

7

"But Mom, I'm a vampire hunter!"

"Okay, Hubie, but you need to eat your dinner."

"I'm not hungry, Mom."

8

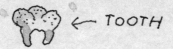 ← TOOTH

"Then brush your teeth and go to bed."

"Aw, Mom. I'm not tired."

"Well, get in bed, and you can read for a while. But none of that horror junk."

CHAPTER 2
A CRYPTIC MESSAGE

It's humiliating for a vampire hunter to go to bed so early. Vampires get to stay up all night. I guess they don't have moms.

Maybe if I slip under the covers and pretend to be asleep, it will fool Mom.

I slip under the covers . . . into a dark tomb. It belongs to Count Dracula. I feel my way along the cold, wet walls. Suddenly, I bump into something. It's a coffin. But the lid is off and it's empty.

OUT TO LUNCH C.D.

"Darn," I say. "I missed him again. I should have come earlier. I wonder where he is. Maybe he's at night school or at the blood bank, making a withdrawal."

CHAPTER 3
LUNCHTIME

"I von to suck your blood."

"Knock it off, Eric, and take out your wax fangs."

"But I'm a vampire," Eric announces. He puts his arms out like the Frankenstein monster.

"Eric, you're a real pain in the neck. And don't you have your monsters a little mixed up?"

"Yeah, vell, I know a vampire's favorite holiday."

"Oh yeah?" I said. "What's that?"

"Fangsgiving." Eric laughed.

"Well, I know a vampire's favorite day of the week," I said.

"Vell so do I," said Eric. "Frightday."

FALLING STAR ↘

ARE YOU OK?

"Not bad," I said, "but his favorite, favorite day is Veinsday!"

"I thought it was Toothday," said Freddy.

"Or Moanday," said Penny.

HA, HA, HA.

FREDDY

I'M A RIOT.

PENNY

"Anyway, I have a great lunch today," said Eric.

"What is it?" I asked.

Eric opened his coffin-shaped lunch box. "Tomato juice and *neck*-tarines."

ERIC'S LUNCH BOX →

CHAPTER 4
FUNNY BONES

After lunch, I wasn't feeling so well. My teacher, Mrs. Green, sent me down to see Ms. Hearst, the school nurse. She wasn't in her office. I sat down and waited.

←TONGUE ⊛←PEPPERONI

There was lots to look at. Pictures of all the organs, eyeballs, and other yucky things. It was hard to imagine all that stuff is also inside of me.

FOOT →

There was also a real skeleton hanging in the corner. I waved hello, but the skeleton didn't wave back. But then it did!

"My name's Hubie," I said. "What's yours?"

"You can call me Bone-apart."

"Are you French?"

"No, I'm just dead."

GIVE ME FIVE!

COOL!

FIVE WHAT?

"Would you like to go to France?"

"No, I don't get around much anymore. I just hang out here."

"I know a riddle," I said.

"Awesome," said the skeleton.

"What do skeletons talk on?"

"I give up."

"A bone phone."

"I have a riddle, too," said the skeleton.

"Go for it," I said.

"How do skeletons eat mashed potatoes?"

"I give up. How *do* skeletons eat mashed potatoes?"

"In a grave-y!" said the skeleton, slapping his knee.

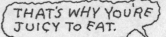

"I have a stomachache," I said.

"I never get stomachaches," said the skeleton. "I don't have a stomach."

"You're lucky," I smiled.

21

The nurse walked back into the office. "I'm sorry to keep you waiting, Hubie."

"That's okay. Your skeleton is really special. He's very debonair."

"Thank you, Hubie, but we all have one just like it inside of us. Even you."

THE SKELETON IS MISSING A LEG.

CRUNCH!

CHAPTER 5
GOING BATS

BATTING CAGE ↓

After school that day, I had a Little League game. My team, the Missing Socks, was playing the Red Socks. We had a real vumpire and lots of bats. It was my turn at the plate. The count was 2 and 2. The pitcher threw a wild pitch, high and outside.

"Strike three!" shouted the vumpire.

"You're as blind as a bat!" I shouted back.

The vumpire lifted his face mask. "I am a bat," he sneered, showing his long, white fangs.

YIKES!

CHAPTER 6
PARDON ME, BOY. IS THIS THE TRANSYLVANIA STATION?

After practice, my mom came to pick me up in our van. Except it wasn't really our van. It was a carriage. And I wasn't waiting for her at the baseball field. I was standing outside of a train station. There was something strange about it. Of course, there had been something strange about this whole trip. The train had been totally empty, and the conductor punched my ticket . . . with his teeth.

The carriage was strange, too. There were no horses pulling it and the driver was a bat. But I was determined to reach Castle Dracula and finish off the Count.

As we rattled through the dark mountains, I was beginning to think that maybe this was not such a good idea.

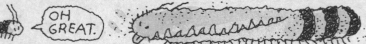

"Hubie, what happened at school today?" Mom snapped me out of it.

BACK TO REALITY →

"There was a vampire in the lunch line and one at the baseball game."

"Hubie, you're going to have to stop daydreaming and focus on your studies. Don't you want to go to college?"

"Maybe night school," I smile.

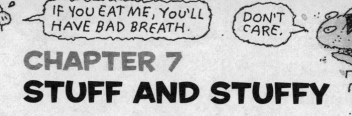

CHAPTER 7
STUFF AND STUFFY

"Hubie, clean up your room before dinner. It's a total mess. Open the windows and let a little air in. It's as stuffy as a tomb," Mom said.

"I like it this way," I answered. "What's for dinner?"

"Your favorite—spaghetti with garlic."

"Great! Put in tons of garlic."

"Hubie, no one will want to come near you."

"Great!" I smiled.

GARLIC HAS A DISTINCT ODOR BUT IMPROVES THE TASTE OF FOOD.

After dinner, I went back to my room. I had taken every precaution possible. I had an extra helping of garlic at dinner, and I was wearing a necklace made of garlic cloves.

As the trip continued, the mountains grew steeper, the night grew darker, and the wolves cried louder. I was having second thoughts. Then the carriage stopped!

AAAOOOOOOO
AAAOOOOOOO

BURP!

I opened the door and stepped out. There I was alone in front of Castle Dracula. I climbed the stone steps—there were a lot of them—and stood in front of a great oak door. There was a sign: We gave at the office.

I was about to knock, when the huge door creaked open.

PULL ME UP; THE FISH AREN'T BITING.

CHAPTER 8
YOU CAN COUNT ON ME

Mom came in and turned out the light.

"I'll kiss you good night after you brush your teeth. You overdid it with the garlic," she said, closing the door.

CLICK!

Standing in front of me was a guy in the best Halloween costume I had ever seen. He was as pale as chalk. He was dressed all in black, which only made him look whiter. His eyes glowed red and he was wearing bright red lipstick—at least, I thought it was lipstick. He looked like a goth rapper. But the

←TICK

strangest thing about him was his teeth. He was an orthodontist's dream. With his three-inch fangs and overbite, he needed braces badly.

"Vot do you vant?" he moaned.

CHAPTER 9
I LIKE YOUR TYPE—
RH-POSITIVE

"Hubie. Go to sleep right now and no excuses," Mom called into my room on her way to bed.

"Okay, okay, Mom."

"And why are you up this late?"

My mind raced for something to say as I stood in front of the vampire.

"I'm a salesman with a special on suntan lotion."

No.

"I'm selling life insurance."

No.

"I'm taking donations for the Red Cross blood drive."

No.

I finally blurted out, "Trick or treat!"

"Halloween is in October and it's Noveinber," moaned the vampire.

"It took me forever to climb your front steps," I answered.

MIND
RACING

DUST MITE ⟶ .

"Vell come inside and make yourself at home. I am Count Dracula," he moaned, licking his fangs.

CAN I BORROW YOUR WINGS?

SURE, COME CLOSER AND I'LL GIVE THEM TO YOU.

I pulled the covers over my head. I followed the count into the castle. It was almost as messy as my room. There were spider webs everywhere. The count walked right through them, but when I tried to follow, I got all tangled up.

LET ME HELP YOU OUT.

LEVITATING ——→ ○

"Sorry," said the count, "it's the maid's day off."

"Is your mom at home?" I muttered.

"She lives necks-door." The count smiled and licked his fangs again.

"How long have you lived here?" I asked.

"Six hundred years," said the count.

"How do you stay in shape?" I asked.

"I'm on a liquid diet and I do neck exercises every night," smiled the count.

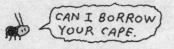

CHAPTER 11
THE HEART OF THE MATTER

There were a lot of rooms in the castle.

"Where's the living room?" I asked.

"We don't have one," smiled the count. "Just a lot of dead space."

BEATING HEART

YUMMY!

I'M ANEMIC.

"A little wallpaper and a couple of football posters would liven things up around here," I said. "Do you like football?"

"I like casketball better," he smiled. "I like to dribble."

"Maybe a rock-and-roll poster. What's your favorite group?"

"The Greatful Dead."

"What are your favorite songs?"

"'Sinking in the Vein' and 'Teeth for Two.'"

"Maybe a travel poster. Do you ever get to travel?"

"I've been to New York City."

"Did you like it?"

"I enjoyed the nightlife. I stayed at the Plazma Hotel and I saw the Vampire State Building."

"What did you think?"

"It's a nice place to visit, but I wouldn't wanna be dead there."

COUNT, THE SUITE I'M GIVING YOU IS DROP-DEAD GORGEOUS.

I LOVE IT ALREADY.

CHAPTER 12
NECKS TO NOTHING

My stomach rumbled. I guess I really overdid the garlic.

"Are you hungry?" asked Count Dracula.

"No, are you?" I asked.

"Actually, I'm Romanian," he answered.

"No, no. Are you hungry? Did I interrupt your dinner?"

LET ME GO!

DON'T SPEAK TO ME WHILE I'M EATING.

"No, you arrived just in time. I'll catch a bite in a little while. I'll get something on the run . . . I like fast food."

"I could come back later," I said.

"No, no," said the count. "Stay the night . . . or longer."

CHAPTER 13
THE TRANSYLVANIA TRANSFORMER

In the middle of the night I woke up and closed the window . . . it was cold. There was something in my room. It was a bat that slowly transformed into the count. His black wings unfolded and became a cape. His fangs grew longer, and his eyes glowed red. I held up the garlic, and he backed away. I guess he's not Italian.

YOU CAN REST ON MY TONGUE.

THANKS!

"I thought I would look in on you," he hissed quietly. "Anything you'd like—a bedtime story, a glass of water, a transfusion?"

"No thanks, I'm good," I answered.

"Vell, sveet dreams," he said, opening the window and turning back into a bat.

If I had a racket, I could have played batminton.

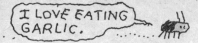
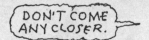
CHAPTER 14
A STAKE IN HIS FUTURE

The next morning, the sun shined brightly through my window. I got out of bed. I didn't brush my teeth. In fact, I had three pieces of garlic for breakfast. I went to the freezer and pulled out a steak. It was a T-bone—I wasn't taking any chances. I started for the basement door, steak in hand.

YOUR WINGS FELL OFF. NOT AGAIN!

KEEP AN EYE OUT FOR MOM.
THEN THAT WILL LEAVE ME WITH ONLY ONE.

WHY ARE YOU HERE?
BECAUSE I'VE BEEN COFFIN ALL DAY.

The castle was empty. All the black curtains were closed. I flung them all open and started down the basement stairs. Luckily, I had brought a flashlight. The lower I went down, the darker it got. I found myself in a creepy, little room.

In the center of the room was a coffin—a very fancy mahogany one with brass handles. I tried to lift the lid. It was very heavy.

I found a board to use as a lever and slowly pried the lid off. There he was, snug as a bug in a rug—his pale hands folded on his chest. He was sound asleep, but he wasn't breathing. I carefully lifted his arms back, when his eyes burst open.

I hit him with the steak. He grabbed my hand in a powerful grip. Then I shined the light in his eyes. He covered his face and made a gurgling growl. I drove the steak into his heart. He gurgled again, lay back down, and finally died.

CHAPTER 15
IN A LIGHTER VEIN

"Go out for a walk, Hubie. You've been in all morning," Mom called into my room.

I left Castle Dracula. The sun was shining and the air was brisk.

As I headed down the mountain toward the train station, I felt good. There was one less bad sucker in the world. The villagers were happy to hear that the Count was finally dead, but some were worried that the sale of garlic would drop off sharply.

Oh well, it's all in a day's work for a vampire hunter.

HISTORY OF THE MYTH OF VAMPIRES

There are many vampires in fiction, but fortunately, none in reality. However, in the animal kingdom, they are quite common. You may have already met mosquitos, fleas, lice, and ticks. They are all little Draculas.

Fortunately, other larger blood suckers are quite rare. Vampire bats, the vampire finch, and lampreys all live off of blood.

DID YOU HEAR THAT THUMP!

The story of Dracula was created by Bram Stoker in his 1897 Gothic novel by the same name. It was inspired by a real person, Prince Vlad, who lived in a castle in Romania. He did not drink blood but was a very unpleasant person. Luckily for us, there are many beverages that are more refreshing and more nourishing than our neighbors' hemoglobin.

BRAM STOKER →